Emily and the
BIG BAD
Bunyip

Written by JACKIE FRENCH

Illustrated by BRUCE WHATLEY

First published in hardback in Australia by HarperCollins Publishers Pty Ltd in 2008
First published in paperback in Great Britain by HarperCollins Children's Books in 2009

10 9 8 7 6 5 4 3 2 1

ISBN: 978-0-00-732427-9

HarperCollins Children's Books is a division of HarperCollins Publishers Ltd.

Visit our website at: www.harpercollins.co.uk
Printed and bound in China

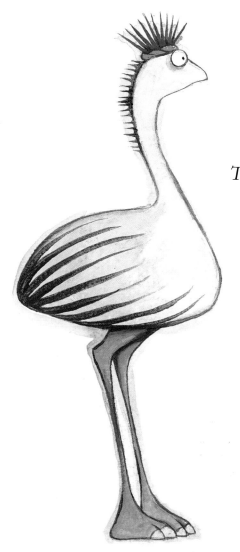

To everyone who loves wombats, emus, kangaroos ...

... and bunyips too.

It was Christmas Day in Shaggy Gully.

The kangaroos were bouncy.

The echidnas were being prickly.

The emus were feeling peckish.

The koalas were eating gumtree leaves

– because that's what koalas do best.

The bats

and possums

were just hanging about.

The cockatoos crooned and the kookaburras
chortled in tune as carols rang out through the bush.

'Dingle dingle dingle,' jingled Ringo the Dingo.

'ZAPPA ZAPPA ZAPPA,' rapped the Christmas beetles' drums.

'Bluuuuurt...' began Emily Emu's tuba.

Suddenly a ghastly
groan floated up from
Shaggy Gully Creek.

I'm MAD and I'm MEAN!
I'm the BUNYIP!

'Ooooogggggghhhhhh!

Oooooooooogggggghhhhhh!'

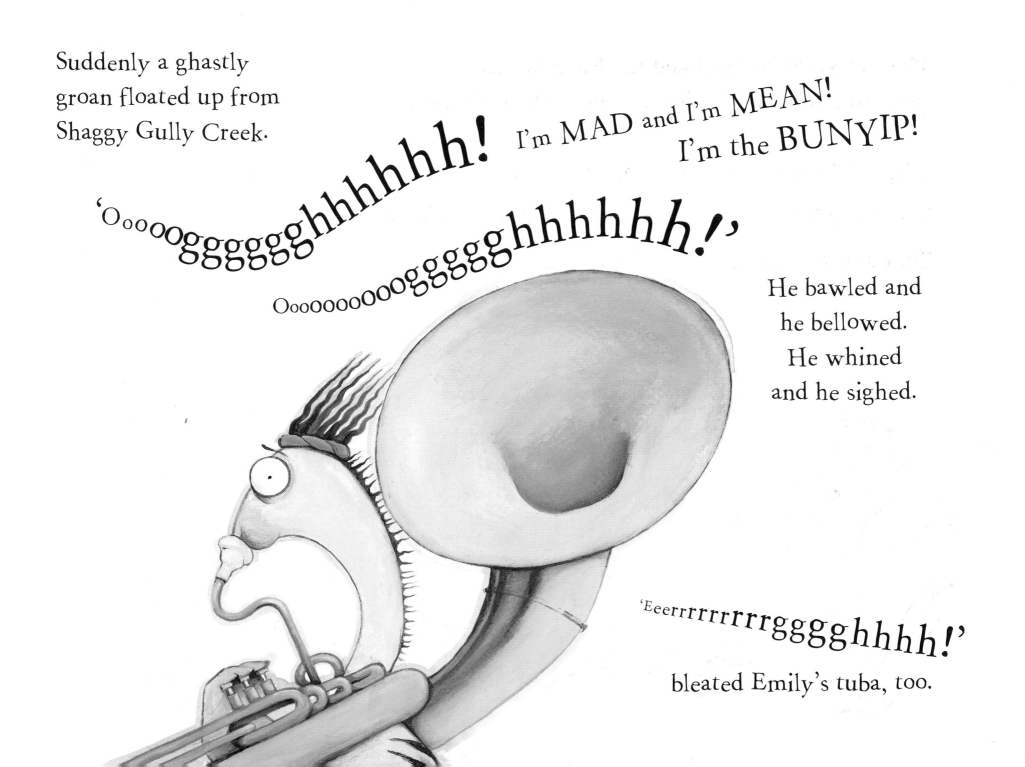

He bawled and
he bellowed.
He whined
and he sighed.

'Eeerrrrrrrrgggghhhh!'

bleated Emily's tuba, too.

'Do try to stay in tune, Emily...'
sighed Miss Dawn, conductor
of the Shaggy Gully Chorus.

'Sorry, but that bunyip moan makes
my tuba groan,' explained Emily.

'Bunyips always howl and scare people,'
said Miss Dawn, shrugging.

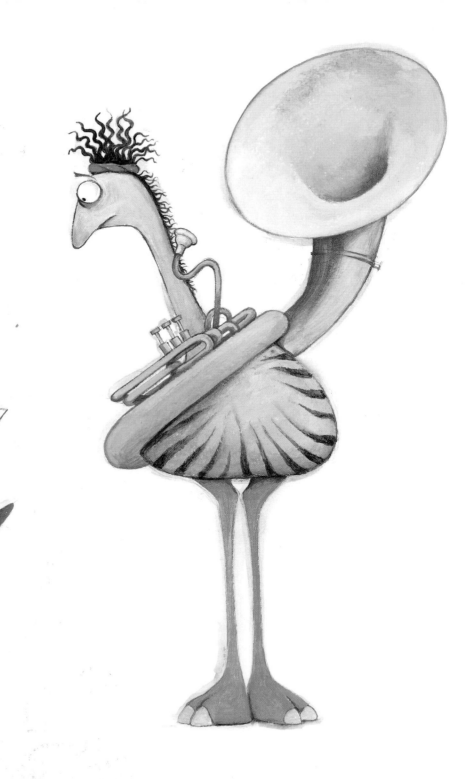

'But it's Christmas!' exclaimed Emily.

'Even a bunyip should smile
on Christmas Day!'

The Shaggy Gully Chorus ran down to the creek.
'Bunyip!' called Emily. 'It's CHRISTMAS
– we're here to make you smile!'

A bellow rose from the water.

'Go away!
I'm mad and I'm mean!
I'm the Bunyip!'

Emily took no notice. Suddenly a giant
shape surged out of the creek.

He was green.

He was wet.

He was big.

He was the Bunyip.

And he wasn't smiling.

'We'll make you a Christmas tree!'
announced Emily.

'Aaaaaaaagggggggghhhhhhh,

I'm mad and I'm mean!
I don't want a Christmas tree!'
yowled the Bunyip.

Emily took no notice.
In no time at all,
a Christmas tree grew before him.

But the Bunyip
did not smile …

'I know what you need,' exclaimed Emily. 'Some Christmas dinner!'

'Eeeeeeeerrrrkkkkk,' bawled the Bunyip.

'I'm MAD and I'm MEAN!
I don't want any Christmas dinner!'

Emily took no notice.

Ringo the Dingo brought his biggest bone.

The Chorus fetched their wiggliest worms.

The koalas brought gumtree leaves

(because that's what koalas do best).

But still the Bunyip didn't smile …

'Christmas presents make everyone smile,' declared Emily.

'Nnnnnaaaaaaaaahhhhh,'

thundered the Bunyip.

'I'm mad and I'm mean!
I'm a bunyip!
Bunyips DON'T like Christmas!
No presents!'

Emily took no notice.
One by one, all the animals brought
a special present for the Bunyip.

But STILL the Bunyip didn't smile!

6 FREE
FLYING LESSONS

B

'What do we do now?' wondered Ringo the Dingo.
Emily's feathers drooped. 'I don't know. Maybe we could
play him one last carol.'

The Shaggy Gully Chorus began to play.
'Dingle dingle dingle,' tingled Ringo the Dingo.
'ZAPPA ZAPPA ZAPPA,' rapped the Christmas beetles' drums.

'Ooommpaoommmpaooooohhhh,'

wailed Emily's tuba sadly.

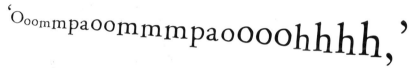

Suddenly…

The Bunyip smiled.

And then he beamed.

And then he LAUGHED ALOUD.

'What's that sound?' he cried.

'That's just my tuba,' apologised Emily.

'I can't play in tune today.'

'It's the most horrible,
terrifying noise I've ever heard.
I LOVE IT!'

shouted the Bunyip.

He grabbed Emily's tuba
and began to play.

'Booooooooooooooooooooooooohhhhhhhhhhhhhh!' blared the tuba.

'Ooooohhh,' moaned the Shaggy Gully Chorus,
as the tuba yowled and howled…
…and shivered and quivered…
…and shrieked and screeched.

'That's the scariest,
gloomiest and
MOST hideous
noise EVER!'
they cried.

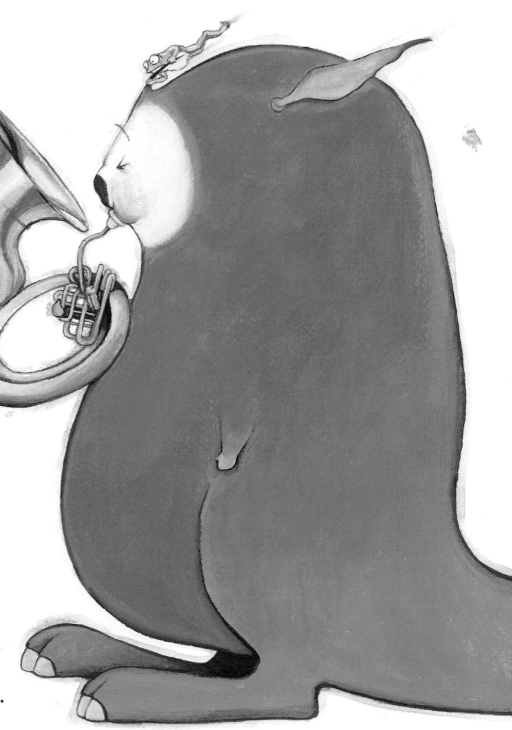

'YES, isn't it!'

hollered the Bunyip happily.

'It's what I've always wanted!'

'So THAT'S what bunyips like!' said Emily.

It was Christmas Day in Shaggy Gully.

The kangaroos bounced.

The emus pecked.

The bats and possums just hung about.

While up from the creek came the most
growling and yowling
... squawking and squalling ...
RACKET in the WORLD!

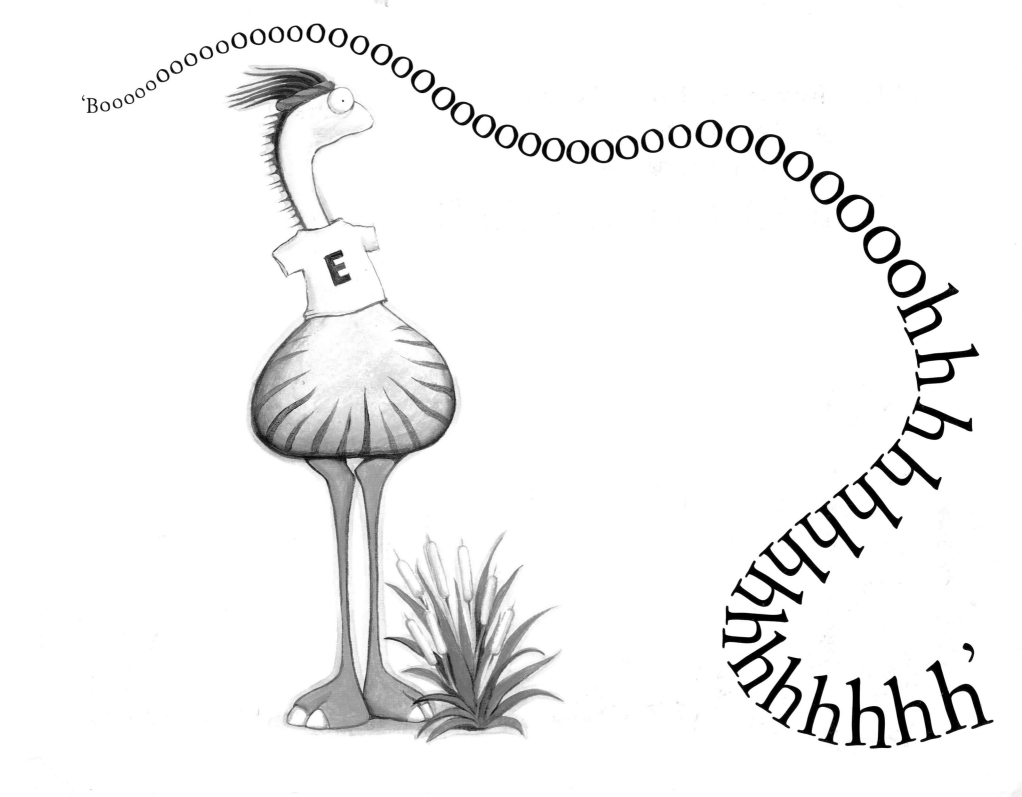